WHEN SUN RULED THE LAND

First-Start® Legends

WHEN SUN RULED THE LAND

A STORY FROM CUBA

Retold by Janet Palazzo-Craig

Illustrated by Dave Albers

Troll

ong ago, Earth lived with her children, Sun and Moon. One day, Earth was tired. She said, "Sun, you will rule the day. Moon, you will rule the night." Then Earth fell asleep.

It was not long before Sun wanted someone to praise him. He took sand and clay. From them, he shaped the first man. Sun breathed life into the man.

The man opened his eyes and bowed before Sun. Sun named him Hamao.

Hamao soon made friends with the animals of Earth. But after a while, he grew sad. "I am lonely," said Hamao to Moon.

Moon knew what to do. She poured a bit of magic dew from a jar. She blew into the dew. A cloud took shape. It was the first woman. Her name was Guanaroca.

"Oh, Moon, she is beautiful!" said Hamao.

Hamao and Guanaroca grew to love each other. In time, they had a son. They named him Imao.

Moon was happy to see the new baby. But Sun was jealous. He decided to take the baby.

So Sun wrapped Moon in thick clouds. Then he took Imao to a mountaintop.

The hungry baby cried for his mother.

As she slept, Guanaroca heard the baby cry. She awoke and reached for him. "Hamao," she gasped, "our son is gone!"

The two looked everywhere. But they could not find him. Soon all the animals joined the search.

At last, a bird spotted the baby.
Sun spit fiery flames at the bird
each time it tried to reach Imao.
The bird decided to wait for Sun to
set.

Hours passed, but Sun would
not leave the sky.

The bird found Guanaroca and told her where Imao was. "Who will save my child?" she cried.

Wind heard her and blew away the clouds around Moon.

Moon awoke. "I will save Imao," she said.

Together, Moon and Wind raced across the hot sky. "Give me the baby," Moon called to Sun. "It is time for night to fall, and I am the ruler of the night."

"No!" shouted Sun.

Moon filled her jar with seawater. She threw the water at Sun.

Sun and Moon battled. Sun threw raging flames. Moon threw water to put out the fire. As they fought, Wind carried away the baby.

Amid the noise, Earth awoke from her long sleep. "Sun," said Earth, "you have broken your promise to share the sky with Moon. See what you have done!"

Sun looked at the pain and fear he had caused. He was ashamed. And so the battle ended.

Moon came forward and stood in front of Sun. Darkness fell on Earth.

But Hamao and Guanaroca suddenly grew afraid. Would Sun ever shine again? "Please, Earth," they cried, "bring back Sun. We cannot live without him."

Slowly, Sun came back into the sky. Then he set in the west. It was Moon's turn to rule.

Moon gave the baby back to Guanaroca and Hamao. Then Moon poured dew from her jar to heal the scars where the battle had been.

To this day, Sun always
shares the sky with Moon.
But if Sun grows restless,
Moon steps before him to
remind him of his promise.
That is what we call an eclipse.

The Caribbean Islands

Florida

Cuba

When Sun Ruled the Land is a legend from the Caribbean island of Cuba. It is a "why" story. A "why" story seeks to explain something that happens in nature. In this case, the story explains how day and night came to be, as well as how the first eclipse took place.